C. H. N. Thomas

The Lady Evelyn

And other Poems

C. H. N. Thomas

The Lady Evelyn
And other Poems

ISBN/EAN: 9783337122799

Printed in Europe, USA, Canada, Australia, Japan

Cover: Foto ©Andreas Hilbeck / pixelio.de

More available books at **www.hansebooks.com**

THE LADY EVELYN

AND OTHER POEMS

BY

MRS. C. H. N. THOMAS

BUFFALO
CHARLES WELLS MOULTON
1895

CONTENTS.

THE LADY EVELYN

THE RHYME OF THE LADY EVELYN.

FORTH from the castle-gate one day,
 Rode Evelyn, the fair,
With Count Alberti at her side—
 A young and lovely pair.

Then spake the Lady Evelyn,
 With laughter and with jest,
"To follow where I lead, Sir Count,
 Shall be of love the test.

"'Tis thus, the gallant knight who weds
 With Evelyn must woo ;"
And with her gloved and dainty hand
 She waved a mock adieu.

Now up the cliff and down the gorge,
 Rash Evelyn has passed,
And after her on trusty steed
 Alberti followed fast.

They rode far down the valley wide,
 And into the green wood,
Unheeding where, until within
 A gypsy camp they stood.

9

Poor Evelyn with wild dismay,
    Turned to Alberti then,
For round the fire of blazing logs
    Stood twenty nut-brown men,

Who menaced them with gesture fierce,
    Till, from a tent hard by,
A maiden, young as Evelyn
    Came gliding silently.

Her cheek was like the berries brown,
    With crimson shining through,
Her teeth like pearls, her eyes and hair
    Were of the midnight hue.

Then Count Alberti's cheek did blanch
    But Evelyn grew strong ;
The men did clamor, fierce and loud,
    " This man hath done us wrong !

"And for that wrong he sure shall die,
    We will avenge our queen !"
The maiden frowned, but nearer drew,
    And spake to Evelyn;

"Fear not, fair lady, I am skilled
    To read the book of fate;
Know thou, from thence, the dove should ne'er
    With the wild vulture mate.

"For him who once betrays his trust
  Is worthy knighthood o'er,
And he who loves, and changes oft,
  Is scorned forever more."

Then to Alberti; "Traitor thou !
  False, shifting as the sand !
Thou knowest the fate my men decree—
  Thy life is in my hand.

"I give it back to thee once more;
  The cup I'd have thee drain,
Yet take heed to thy steps, nor dare
  To cross my path again !

"And now, away, from out my sight,"
  The gipsy cried, " be gone ! "
Alberti turned and Evelyn
  Rode home that day alone.

And never more, from that sad hour,
  Did any mount her steed;
And never more did Evelyn
  To lover's vows give heed.

She gave her wealth unto the church,
  Abjured earth's love and pride;
And sought, within a convent's wall,
  To be Heaven's worthy bride.

A SAILOR'S STORY.

MY home was on the mountain side,
   I ne'er had seen the sea,
But ev'ry tale of ocean life
   I read most eagerly.

I fashioned mimic ships and boats
   Like the pictures I had seen,
And played with them, while others played
   Upon the village green.

I learned the songs the sailors sung
   About the " deep blue sea,"
And said, that when I grew a man,
   A sailor I would be !

My mother's face grew pale, for her
   The ocean had no charms,
And she would wake with shivering dread,
   And fold me in her arms.

I was not strong and stalwart
   Like my brothers, Rob and John,
And so they planned a scholar's life
   For me, the youngest one.

They would go out into the world
  And win their daily bread,
While I with mother should remain
  And stand in father's stead.

I studied much and studied long,
  Lest I should give them pain,
And in that time I learned to love
  My little neighbor, Jane.

I loved them all, and yet my thoughts
  Were ever of the sea,
By day, by night, awake, asleep,
  I heard its melody.

And then, I think, my brain grew wild
  And I could bear no more ;
I fled, nor stayed my feet until
  I heard the ocean's roar.

I loved them all, and yet I left
  Without a parting word,
And sailed the sea exultingly
  As any uncaged bird.

My soul was sated with delight,
  I roamed the wide world o'er ;
We touched at many a fertile isle,
  And many a desert shore.

We traded much from port to port,
   And much I found my gain ;
"And soon I shall go home," I said,
   "And marry little Jane."

How shall I tell what followed,
   Of storm and wreck at sea ?
How shall I tell of long, long years
   Of sad captivity ?

I reached my mountain home at last,
   A weary man and worn,
Unknowing and unknown, I sat
   In the cot where I was born.

A stranger's fire was on the hearth,
   And none a welcome gave,
For Rob and John were far away,
   My mother in her grave.

Jane was a thrifty farmer's wife,
   With children at her knee ;
I would not mar her happiness
   With any thought of me.

I stood, a beggar, at her door,
   She waited my command,
I humbly asked a little bread,
   And took it from her hand.

She pitied me and she was kind ;
  What could I ask for more?
And with a murmured word of thanks
  I left her cottage door.

My home is now upon the wave,
  Naught else remains to me ;
And when this wasted life shall end,
  Bury me in the sea.

A WOMAN'S STORY.

A LITTLE woman, worn and old,
Sat by her cottage door,
With folded hands upon her lap,
Her knitting on the floor.

The playful kitten, at its will
Entangled still the yarn ;
The good man came with shuffling step
From out the low roofed barn.

Unnoted by the musing dame,
Whose thoughts were far away,
Until the noisy boys came in,
Each from his work or play,

And for their supper clamored loud,
Showing the ample store
Of pearly eggs that they had found,
And milk pail brimming o'er.

Then she arose, with quiet step,
Clad in her sober gown,
And brought for them the wheaten loaf
And placed beside the brown.

16

With cheese and butter from the kine
  That browsed upon the hill,
And poured with careful hand the milk
  Each urchin's cup to fill.

With many a merry joke and laugh
  The humble feast sped on,
The mother watched with smiling eyes
  Until the last was done.

Then for a space they sat and talked—
  The patient dog was fed—
The clock struck nine, and soon the boys
  Went lingeringly to bed.

Upon his straight and high-backed chair
  The good man sat and dozed,
The almanac he tried to scan,
  Upon his lap lay closed.

The yellow mug of cider stood
  Near by his toil-worn hand,
The candle faintly blazed and flared
  Upon the little stand.

The daily care, the washing of
  Each platter and each cup,
Was over, and the good wife took
  Her thoughts and knitting up.

"I wonder why my heart to-night
  Should be so strangely stirred
With thoughts of one who left us all
  Without a parting word?

"I wonder if he ever knew,
  Or if he thought it wrong,
That John and I should wed, when we
  Had thought him dead so long?

"I wonder if he ever heard
  How with us all it fared?
That his poor mother, in her age
  Our home and fortune shared?

"I gave an old man at the gate
  A little food to-day,
And, mayhap, something in his look
  Recalled lost Willie Gray.

"Recalled him, but the dream has lost
  It's power to vex my life,
And I have been for many years
  A loyal, loving wife.

"And though, together, in our lot
  Sorrow and joy be blent,
I rest in his enduring love,
  I rest and am content."

The clock struck ten ; its noisy whirr
   Awakened John from sleep,
And roused the dog, its nightly watch
   And faithful ward to keep.

The moonlight flooded all the room,
   And glorified the pair,
Who knelt together in the hush
   And breathed their evening prayer.

GERTRUDE LANE.

AN OLD MAN'S STORY.

IT is a dreary night of wind and storm,
　And I, an old man, bent with many years,
Would tell a tale of one whose life has been
Darkened with crime and swept with passion's
　　winds.
Old mem'ries stir within my heart to-night,
I may be garrulous, but shall not swerve
From simple truth.　You all know Gertrude Lane,
"Crazed Gertrude" you do call her.　Your alms-
　　house
For years has been her prison.　I knew her
In her childhood.　Together oft we played
Beneath the old red farm-house's sloping roof,
Or she stood watching by, the while I climbed
Up the great rafters of the old brown barn
For swallow's nests; she, crying for the birds,
Yet proud of my success.　I marked for her
Each sunny spot where the wild strawberry grew,
And shook the first ripe apples from the bough,
And plucked the purple clusters of the grape.

When tired of rambling, on the vine-wreathed
    porch
We curled the long, smooth dandelion stems
To mimic ringlets; or, with berries red
Plucked from the alder and the wintergreen,
Made coral necklaces.   So childhood fled.

Her father held an office high in church,
A man most pious, orthodox, austere,
And Gertrude knew no end of psalms and hymns,
And in her catechizing never failed.
'Twas sweet to see the grace with which she filled
The place of her dead mother.   Household ways
And homely duties borrowed charms from her.

The gaping country youth opened their eyes
In dull amazement as she glided down
The long aisle of the village church, behind
Her old rheumatic father with his cane!
The breeze just lifted her brown curls, and played
With the blue, floating ribbons of her hat,
And swept her white robe into graceful folds,
If e'er one spark of vanity or pride
Did lurk within that good man's pious heart,
'Twas Gertrude called it forth.   And she was proud
She knew her beauty and the power it gave,
And loved its exercise.   No mother's voice
Taught her the beauty of humility,

And so the rank weeds grew within her heart
And choked the flowers, until she looked with scorn
Upon her lot in life and humble friends;
I was the last—but she did give me up.

Her hour of triumph and of trial came.
A stranger to our hamlet found his way,
A man of wealth, but base and dissolute,
Who, pleased with Gertrude's beauty, tarried till
The summer passed, and its green foliage
Put on autumnal glories.   Then Gertrude
Was left, to watch and wait for his return.
Days grew to weeks—weeks lapsed to months—
        and still
He came not, and poor Gertrude's face grew wan
And white with terror, till, one winter night,
When the first snow was whitening all the fields,
She fled her father and her childhood's home!
The weak old man, stunned by the blow, spoke not,
But feebly moaned, and stretched his withered
        hands
As if in search of something lost; then died,
And the old house passed into stranger's hands.

The years rolled on, and Gertrude's name was
        heard
Only when uttered by some warning voice.
One day, while in the city, I did stroll

nto a crowded court-room.   The pris'ner
Vas a woman, charged with some high misdeed,
\nd as the judge dwelt on each circumstance
\nd pointed out each aggravating fact,
n words that *leaned not unto Mercy's side,*
 turned and looked upon her—Gertrude Lane!
)h Heaven! could that be Gertrude? so bold and
     bad,
Vith such unshrinking eyes and painted face,
 heard them doom her to a prison cell—
\1y childhood's playmate—friend of riper years.
she listened undismayed, but clenched her hands
\nd muttered something in the judge's ear.

"he years passed on, and Gertrude Lane came
     forth
nto the world again, white-haired and bent,
' Hateful and hating," without home or friends,
n her despair, she sought the home of him
Vho was at once her judge and her betrayer,
\nd begged of him, for charity's sweet sake,
\ome humble shelter; but he blandly smiled
\nd pointed to the almshouse.   Gertrude, then,
\aising her tall form to its fullest height,
\nd clasping her thin hands, did call on God
"o judge between them, with such anguished look
\nd bitter words, that the stern judge recoiled
\ghast. *He knew her then,* and his white lips

Did whisper Gertrude!   But she heeded not,
And the proud man turned on his heel and sought
His palace home.   A raving maniac
Was found upon the street next day, and brought
To the cold shelter of the almshouse walls.

One day, the judge, taking his daily ride,
Reined his fine horses at the humble gate,
For he, by virtue of his office, clothed
With due authority, those wretches made
His special care, and daily thanked his God,
That he was not, like them, a sinner vile.
His young wife, reclined on velvet cushions,
And toying with a fair boy's golden curls
Awaited his return; at heart, meanwhile,
Praising her husband's large benevolence,
And charity, that prompted him to look
On scenes which her refined fastidiousness
Shrank from with loathing.   And when he came
     forth
Haggard and pale, she gently chided him
That he did look upon such shocking things,
She knew not of his sin, nor knew she aught
Of Gertrude Lane; but that last interview
Will haunt his memory until death.

ONLY A BEGGAR.

THE beggar lay dead by the roadside,
  A pitiful sight to see,
But then he was only a beggar,
  And nothing to you or me.

He was only a common beggar,
  An old man, haggard and thin,
Who had lived for years on the bounty,
  Oft grudged by his fellow men.   •

His gray hair, all matted and tangled,
  Was wet with the evening dew,
But then he was only a beggar
  And nothing to me or you.

He was weary and worn with travel,
  His feet could no further go
In chase of the beautiful phantom
  That beckoned from " long ago."

With eyes, like the eyes of the maiden,
  Full of gentleness and truth,
Who died on the morn of her bridal,
  The love of his long-lost youth,

And left him so crazed and heart-broken,
  To wander alone through life,
Its joys and its pleasures unheeding,
  Unheeded its turmoil and strife.

He was bronzed with the suns of summer,
  He was pinched with winter's cold,
His fare was but scanty and meager,
  He sought no silver or gold,

Nor honors from men ; but still onward
  With eager and restless tread,
Never turning aside one moment,
  He keeps his tryst with the dead !

How gently the moonlight is falling
  On the forehead, white and bare,
And the hands that were clasped in passion,
  Are folded as if in prayer !

The eyes look above and beyond us,
  And beauty we can not see
Is vouchsafed to the beggar's vision,
  But hidden from you and me.

Let him rest in the pauper's corner,
  Whose stones are mossy and grim,
For earth with its show and its honor,
  Is nothing now unto him !

EDITH GRAY.

OH, Edith Gray, I've loved you well,
    Yet why should I the tale rehearse?
Full well I know that you would scorn
    Alike the singer and his verse.

For I am a poor poet born,
    My idle rhymes my only boast;
Your father sits with merchant kings,
    His vessels trade on every coast.

And day by day, and hour by hour,
    He seeks for you a worthy mate;
But worthiness he finds alone
    Among the titled and the great.

And I, a poet, poor but proud
    As any prince in all the land,
Might vainly plead, sweet Edith Gray,
    And vainly sue for your white hand.

If, in a serving-man's estate,
    I might but look on your fair face,
List to the rustle of your robe,
    And the soft flutter of your lace ;

EDITH GRAY.

If in such mean and humble guise,
  I thus might worship from afar,
I would accept and bless the lot,
  Guided and ruled by one bright star.

But far away, mid other scenes,
  To which my heart will give slight heed,
With throbbing brow and tortured brain,
  On some fair morning, I shall read

Details of splendor and of pomp,
  With which a bride was given away,
And glancing down the page, the name
  Of my lost love—sweet Edith Gray!

LEGEND OF LAKE ALEXANDER.

TWO miles in length and one in breadth,
  Lake Alexander lieth,
Far to the south, one little isle
  The traveler espieth.

Loon Island, its euphonious name,
  Its shores are fringed with rushes,
While farther in grow scrubby oaks
  And whortleberry bushes.

And yet, this island, lone and bare,
  Hath place in old tradition,
Linked with the red-man's name and fame,
  And with his superstition.

It was a mountain's summit once
  According to the story;
A mountain grand, which stood alone
  In solitary glory.

29

And hither came the Indian tribes,
  From miles around they gathered,
Each dusky brave, as fancy pleased,
  Bepainted and befeathered.

The morn beheld their sacred rites,
  Their festal scenes each even,
Night after night, to revelry
  And song and dance were given.

Alas for them, like wiser men,
  They tired of simple pleasures,
And to increase their wanton mirth
  Devised new means and measures.

Strange panic seized that guilty crowd,
  They paused in their mad revel,
And offered human sacrifice
  To Maniton and devil !

Then the Great Spirit angry grew,
  The sky shook with his thunder,
The mountain trembled 'neath their feet,
  The earth was rent asunder.

Majestic, slow, the mountain sank
  Down to its very summit,
And every living thing was drowned
  That chanced to be upon it,

Save one old squaw upon the top,
  Weeno whose voice of warning
Fell on her people's ears each day,
  But met with only scorning.

She stood, the last of all her race,
  Her lonely lot bewailing,
Till o'er the lake, one summer night,
  A wierd canoe came sailing.

The oarsman was a dusky chief
  Of high and noble station,
And Weeno sailed away with him
  To her own tribe and nation,

Unto the happy hunting ground
  Which all the good inherit,
Beyond the farthest setting sun,
  Prepared by the Great Spirit.

LIZZIE LEE.

GOOD-morning, sir, your name is Paul Brown,
  My mem'ry's good you see;
Your father—he was the village 'squire,
  You married Lizzie Lee.

She was the miller's girl, poor and proud
  As maiden well could be,
You tempted her with your shining gold
  And she proved false to me.

I cursed you then in my boyish wrath,
  With curses loud and deep,
For many a year I nursed my hate,
  And would not let it sleep.

I've traveled many a mile by land,
  And many leagues by sea,
And my only hope in life has been
  To forget Lizzie Lee.

Vain were my efforts—with brain half crazed,
  Weary and sick I come,
You need not fear me; I only wish
  To die in peace at home.

Do not tell Lizzie, but let me go
    A-begging to your door,
And crave a morsel from that white hand,
    That I may clasp no more !

Nay, let me kiss it—one kiss of thanks,
    Why start you in alarm ?
She'll think me a crazy vagabond,
    'Twill sure do you no harm.

Your sons are stately, your daughters fair,
    I will not them offend,
They shall not know that the beggar man
    Was once their mother's friend!

I would look upon your princely home
    And on your acres broad;
Your plans have prospered; for all your toil
    You reap a large reward.

You are rich in gold and rich in gear
    And rich in Lizzie Lee:
I envy you not, but do rejoice
    In your prosperity.

When the snow shall whiten the hillside
    The bell will toll some day
Proclaiming the soul of the beggar
    Hath passed from earth away.

Then come to the cot on the hillside,
    Take with you Lizzie Lee,
And tell her this tale of her lover—
    Tell of his constancy.

Perhaps she will gaze on me kindly,
    Beautiful Lizzie Lee!
Perhaps she will touch my forehead,
    Call me " poor fool " maybe!

If one tear shall fall from those blue eyes,
    The bitter past to drown,
'Twill cancel all, and there shall be peace
    'Twixt you and me, Paul Brown.

REMINISCENCE.

JOANNA dear, do you forget
   This was our wedding day?
Just forty years ago, my love,
   Just such a morn of May.

Lay by your knitting, come and sit
   Beneath this old oak tree,
And let us talk of all the past
   Has brought to you and me.

I see you now in muslin white,
   White roses in your hair,
And pink ones on your cheeks, my love,
   Now wan and pale with care.

A year passed on, and in my arms
   Our first born child was laid;
I, of its long and flowing robes
   And helplessness, afraid.

A feeble, wailing, sickly thing,
   We loved him all the more;
And as he faded, day by day,
   Our hearts grew sad and sore.

Then Bessie came—our merry one—
    Black eyed and raven haired,
So full of life and joyousness,
    We dreamed she would be spared

To comfort us in our old age,
    To be our staff and stay,
But fever smote her in a night,
    She withered in a day!

And then came God's last crowning gift,
    Our twin boys, good and brave,
They grew in beauty and were all
    Our fondest wish could crave.

E'en unto manhood's strength they grew,
    And with them grew our pride,
Our country called, and in her ranks
    Our boys stood side by side.

They faltered not—through fire and smoke
    Shoulder to shoulder stood;
They faltered not, while all around
    The battlefield ran blood!

The rebel bullets harmed them not,
    Yet one came home to die,
Slain by the unseen foe that lurked
    In Chickahominy.

He died at home, and all was done
  To comfort his last hours;
He died at home—his grave is here—
  We cover it with flowers.

But, for his brother, woe is me
  For all that him befell,
And woe is me that I should live
  The bitter tale to tell.

He died of hunger, in a land
  God crowned with plenteousness;
Day after day, week after week
  A living death was his!

The fiend, starvation, long he held
  With his strong will at bay,
But frost was keen and sharp by night,
  The sun consumed by day.

Death came at last—thank God for that!
  His sufferings are o'er,
Where he has gone, the wicked come
  To trouble him no more.

Peace dawns at last upon the land
  He gave his life to save,
Peace dawns at last, while he is left
  To fill a nameless grave.

'Tis hard to talk of this, dear wife,
But still we murmur not,
For we have learned in ev'ry state,
Contentment with our lot.

And He, who sees the sparrow fall
Will hear us when we pray;
We'll bless the hand that smiteth us
And trust Him though He slay!

WATCHING AND WAITING.

STAY, mariner, stay, for the love of God,
   And tell me what news you bring from the sea,
Have you seen or heard of the " Flying Cloud "
   That bore my true lover away from me?

Ten years ago, on a morning like this,
   He bade me adieu with kisses and tears;
was timid and thought but of danger,
   He was stout-hearted and laughed at my fears.

He promised to come a year from that day,
   And cheerily said, " Will you watch for me ? "
So hither I come with each morning's sun,
   And watch for that good ship coming from sea.

What think you, mariner, when will she come ?
   Have you crossed on the deep her snow track,
Was she homeward bound, or lay she becalmed ?
   Oh, tell me when will my sailor come back ?

The neighbors look sad, with pitying eyes,
   And say that good ship went down long ago;
Have you seen e'er a mast or floating spar ?
   Kind mariner, tell me it is not so.

Tell me she trades in some Indian port,
   In gold, and in gems and in fabrics rare;
Or she lades with the fragrant Chinese herb,
   And soon her rich cargo will homeward bear.

Go, mariner, go you are like the rest,
   You shake your head, and you bid me forget;
I will not beleive so dismal a tale,
   But will watch and wait for my sailor yet!

I must be going; the day weareth on
   That perchance will bring my lover to me;
And I must be there when the "Flyiug Cloud"
   With her sails all spread cometh home from sea!

"TO MARY—AGED SEVENTEEN."

THERE'S a lone grave in the churchyard,
  With head-stone mossy and green,
That beareth only this record,
  " To Mary—aged seventeen."

No hymn or scripture is quoted,
  Her virtues to blazon forth;
The rude stone speaks not of beauty,
  Affection, talent or worth.

All you can learn of her story,
  What she was, or might have been,
Is told in that one brief sentence
  "To Mary—aged seventeen."

Old tradition saith that somewhere
  A child is roving alone;
He claimeth none as his father,
  None claimeth him as a son.

He only knows that his mother
  Died a death of shame and sin,
That all the remembrance of her
  Is, "Mary—aged seventeen"

Far down the street, in his mansion,
　　'Neath his old ancestral trees,
A gray-haired man from youth hath dwelt,
　　Like a patriarch at ease.

His wife is fair, and in his home
　　Seemeth regal like a queen;
Six sons are his—one daughter fair,
　　Named Mary—aged seventeen.

With his warm cloak wrapped about him,
　　Then the old man steals away,
And jostles the pallid stranger
　　Whom he gave an alms that day.

Unheeding all, he wanders on,
　　Though the wind is cold and keen,
Remorse impels him to the grave
　　Of Mary—aged seventeen.

And after him the pale boy walks,
　　On his mother's grave to moan,
Unknowing and unknown to each
　　Meet father and outcast son!

AT REST.

WITHIN the consecrated place, where good
 And loyal Catholics are laid to rest,
'Neath marble tablet or rude cross of wood,
 Alike with folded hands and pulseless breast,

I found a long, low mound o'erspread with grass,
 With tufts of pink each side in formal row,
And at the head and foot a clustered mass
 Of great June roses, red and white, ablow,

And on the cross I read the carven name
 Of one whom I had known in other years,
A weary woman "all unknown to fame,"
 Who ate her bread in bitterness and tears.

An exile from her native land, she pined
 With ceaseless longing for her own "green isle"
Hoping through weary quest her love to find,
 Yet looking back, like Lot's wife, all the while.

Unrest and poverty her husband drove
 A better fortune on our shores to seek,
His mis-spelled letters little held save love,
 She wanted bread, and her stout heart grew weak.

She clasped her children in her arms at length,
　With courage born of love and of despair,
Nerving herself with desperation's strength,
　The unknown perils of the sea to dare.

Bravely the ship sped on, day after day,
　Till one fair morn they reached the goal long-
　　sought,
And up and down they went their weary way,
　And hand to hand, the wolf of hunger fought.

With "hope deferred" her woman's heart grew
　　sick,
　A stranger in a stranger's land was she ;
Why came he not? Her tears fell fast and thick,
　Was it for this she crossed the moaning sea ?

Hard work and scanty fare her lot was still,
　In the new home her children grew and throve,
And day by day, her set tasks to fulfil,
　In sickness and in weariness she strove,

Till mortal sickness seized the feeble frame,
　And the good priest was summoned in her need ;
With pitying eyes and gentle step he came,
　And to her plaint gave loving care and heed,

" Your name ? " and, as she murmured faint and
    weak,
  " My daughter, I have tidings," quickly said,
 " Among the living thou dost vainly seek
    For one long resting with the silent dead !

"In a great hospital I stood by him
    And gave him absolution, full and free ;
His name was thine—with words confused and dim,
    He told the tale that thou hast told to me."

She clasped her hands, as one who findeth rest,
    When years of doubt and of suspense are o'er,
With faith in God, and in her husband blest,
    She turned, as one content, and asked no more,

But waited calmly for her glad release,
    Slipping her rosary through fingers wan,
A saint, and martyr, crowned with joy and peace,
    Instead of earth's despised and outcast one.

The bruised feet tread no more life's weary way,
    Sorrow and pain and mourning are forgot,
Enfolded safe, she waiteth for the day,
    Strange flowers and alien skies she heedeth not.

A CASTLE IN THE AIR.

I BUILT in a Spanish province,
   A castle fair and high,
It rose with tower and battlement
   Against the glowing sky.

In the background lay a forest
   As weird and dark as night,
And over all uprose sublime,
   A snow-capped mountain height.

Upon the lake my gilded boat
   Lay gleaming like a star,
And the commerce of all nations,
   I looked on from afar.

All precious woods and spices rare
   I burnéd for perfume,
My garden held the choicest flowers
   That in the tropics bloom.

Each merry songster of the air
   I caged for my delight,
And every gorgeous bird was there
   With plumage gay and bright.

46

My table groaned beneath the weight
  Of flesh, and fowl, and fish,
My servants sleepless spent the night,
  T' invent some dainty dish.

My couch was of the eider down,
  With silken curtains hung,
And twining vines, and buds, and flowers,
  Seemed o'er my carpets flung.

And I had music of all kinds,
  If pensive or if gay,
The lute, the viol and the harp
  With men well skilled to play.

And dancers came with tinkling feet
  Whenever I did call ;
Cool grottoes wooed to solitude
  When mirthful scenes did pall.

My guests were not of common men,
  Some glory each did crown ;
With pen, or lyre, or battle sword
  They'd won a great renown.

And for this fairy home of mine
  I sought and won a bride,
She was peerless in her beauty
  And nobly born beside.

I lavished my great wealth on her
  With an unsparing hand,
Her silks and diamonds well might match
  With any in the land.

Here my wife came in from shopping,
  The babe began to cry ;
My cigar had burned my fingers,
  The smoke was in my eye.

Wife's talk was about the bonnets
  And things she'd seen down town
And while I mused on the prices
  My castle tumbled down !

HELLO !

WOULD you know the fairest thing I saw
      While wandering up and down
Through the highways and the byways
   Of a pretty country town ?

The very fairest thing I saw
   Was a little child at play;
A chubby, dimpled, laughing child,
   Who sat beside the way,

And with a spoon made pies of sand,
   Placing them in a row ;
Pausing a moment, she looked up,
   And shyly said, "Hello !"

Her head was bare, her feet were bare,
   Her frock was torn and old ;
Soft, tangled curls made round her head
   An aureole of gold.

The fullness of contentment shone
   Within her soft, brown eyes,
Upturned to mine, as smiling still,
   She sat and made her pies.

49

She had no words of love and trust,
  Her baby speech was slow;
Waif of the street, her lisping tongue
  Caught but the word " Hello! "

The sunlight shimmered on her hair,
  And kissed the baby face;
While homely garments round her fell
  With an unconscious grace.

She was too timid to caress,
  Her name I did not know;
What could I do but give her back,
  With smiles, her soft " Hello? "

And pray she might play, undisturbed,
  Through the long summer hours;
Spite of neglect, might grow and thrive
  As did the wayside flowers.

FIFTY YEARS.

Do you remember, David,
  This was our wedding day?
We two, who are so sober now,
  Were then both young and gay.

'Tis fifty years ago, love;
  I was but seventeen—
A simple, rustic maiden,
  But happy as a queen.

Our home has been a happy one,
  But one thing was denied;
The boon for which, like Hannah,
  Unto the Lord I cried.

But from His poor, who through the street
  Unpitied oft do roam,
We singled out a boy and girl,
  And took them to our home.

The boy was winsome, bold and bright,
  The girl was sweet and fair;
I lavished on them, day by day,
  All a fond mother's care.

The lad had seen six summers,
    The girl was turned of four;
We sent them to the village school
    To learn its humble lore.

They mastered all their teachers knew;
    How proud we were, you know,
When John could read and write and spell,
    And Sue could knit and sew.

They grew to youth and maidenhood,
    And left the village school;
We thanked the Lord for his rich gifts,
    And deemed our cnp was full.

Our John grew tall and stalwart,
    And longed to sail the sea,
And when we pleaded with him,
    Grew strange to you and me.

The lad was not our flesh and blood,
    We could not say him "nay!"
Somehow he always had a knack
    Of having his own way.

With breaking hearts, poor Sue and I
    His shirts and jackets made,
And on the pile, when neatly done,
    His little Bible laid.

Gay, joyous letters came at first,
  Such as a boy would write,
And then a gloom of silence fell
  Upon our hearts like night.

We learned at last—ah me!—we learned
  What fate our boy befell;
How his ship went down off Hatteras
  A comrade's pen did tell.

Poor Sue! what could I do or say?
  She neither spoke nor stirred,
But gazed on me with vacant eyes
  As if she heard no word.

I had not dreamed she loved the boy
  Save with a sister's love;
I hushed my own wild grief to soothe
  My stricken, wounded dove.

But the white face on the pillow
  Grew whiter each sad day,
A lily, broken on its stem,
  She drooped and pined away.

We've none to lean on now, David,
  Our lot seems sad and lone;
But still, through grace, we both can say
  " Thy will, O Lord, be done."

THE PHANTOM SHIP.

OH, when will the ship come back,
   The ship that sailed out to sea,
Twenty long years ago, or more,
   Bearing my lover from me?

I am weary with "hope deferred,"
   My soul is sick with pain;
I look where the sky and waters meet,
   But ever I look in vain.

I loved with a jealous madness,
   I scorned with a cruel hate;
But my heart, alas! is broken,
   I have learned the truth too late.

We parted in wrath and anger—
   He spoke not a word to me;
I snatched his ring from my finger
   And tossed it into the sea!

He lies in his fresh, young beauty,
   Asleep in the ocean bed,
With corals and pink shells round him,
   And mosses above him spread.

Mine eyes are heavy with tears—
  With a weight of tears unshed;
My soul is filled with the anguish
  Of a vague and nameless dread.

Oft, when the tempest is raving
  Here on this desolate shore,
Through the mist his bark comes gliding,
  A phantom and nothing more!

And a phantom hand points downward
  Where the ring fell in the sea
And the gleam of its starry sparkle
  Is borne through the depths to me.

CHINESE LILIES.

GO forth upon the street and note the signs
    That stare at you from ev'ry house and wall,
A "Chinese Laundry" with the name "Lee Sing"
   You'll find conspicuous among them all.

"Lee Sing" has gone the way the Chinese go,
   Another fills his place and wears the quaint cos-
      tume,
And in the window, empty once and bare,
   Some creamy, fragrant lilies bud and bloom.

The owner smiles and says "they come from
      home,"
   And "home" I know is half a world away;
Do faces dark, with slanting, almond eyes,
   Haunt his imagination day by day?

Or, does he come and for barbarians toil
   That he may purchase with his increased store,
At low Celestial rate, a wife to be his slave
   And in the "Flowery Kingdom" toil no more?

I'll not believe it; let me dream my dream,
   And weave my romance o'er the lilies fair,
A graceful maid comes tripping on small feet,
   A scent of sandal-wood is in the air!

BROOKLYN BRIDGE IN A FOG.

THE night had been a night of storm,
    And far away
Seemed the fair harbor of New York,
    At break of day.

Enveloped in the densest fog,
    Man's works of pride
Were veiled and hidden from the sight
    On either side.

The fog-horns blew with warning wail,
    And then a cry
Rose to each lip, and upward turned
    Each eager eye.

Was it a filmy web of lace
    Floating in light?
Had fairy artist left his work
    In black and white?

Was Jacob's ladder downward let
　　To earth again,
That angel feet might come and go
　　'Twixt God and man?

Was't a black rainbow, born of fog
　　And morning's ray?
We knew not, but "'Tis Brooklyn Bridge"
　　We heard men say.

BABY'S NAME.

BRING me my "specs" and Bible, wife,
  (The large one on the stand),
I would find the record of my birth,
  Writ in my father's hand.

Upon the yellow leaf, between
  The Scriptures, Old and New;
Three children died in infancy,
  And two to manhood grew.

I had not thought that I was old,
  Although my hair is white,
I feel as fresh and young at heart
  As any boy to-night!

But we *are* getting old, dear wife,
  Forget it as we may;
And you, with your still comely cheek
  Are grandmama to-day.

The prettiest babe I ever saw—
  So cunning, wise and bright—
Although his face was red with rage,
  His small hands clenched for fight!

59

But he will soon learn milder ways,
    And laugh and " coo," and crow,
And day by day, and year by year;
    In strength and stature grow.

All day I've sought a name renowned
    To write upon this page;
But names renowned, o'ershadow oft
    Life's humble heritage.

And so I'll write within this book
    Here just beneath my own,
The name my honored father bore,
    The good old name of " John."

GRANDMA'S PLAY.

D EAR grandma had told every story,
    That in her long life she had known,
To the restless "wee bit" maiden,
    Whose syllabled name was her own.

Elizabeth,—fully and clearly,—
    Not "Lizzie," nor "Bessie," nor "Bess,"
Though sometimes, in froliesome humor,
    We styled them the "greater" and "less."

"Now, grandma, I want you to 'muse me"
    Said Elizabeth, maiden small,
And straightway she brought in her dollies—
    There were five of them in all—

And on grandmamma's lap she laid them,
    Dorothea, and Roxy, and John,
Alice, Maud and Victoria Adelaide—
    Down with measles, every one!

Then grandmamma played, she was doctor,
    And Elizabeth was the nurse;
And with this and with that they dosed them,
    But the dollies grew worse and worse!

Such nursing and tending, before them
  No dollies had ever received,
And over their limp, little figures
  The nurse and the doctor hung, grieved,

Till Elizabeth, watching intently,
  Some sign of "conves'cense" did spy,
(A big word used by her mamma
  One day when the maiden was by).

Then the doctor praised the nurse's care,
  And the nurse praised the doctor's skill;
The two Elizabeths lifted the dolls,
  And threw away powder and pill.

Princesses Alice and Adelaide,
  In their royal robes were dresssed,
While humble Roxy and Dorothea
  Were arrayed in their very best.

John, who was only a "horrid boy,"
  And had but a leg and an arm,
Was gently wrapped in his velvet cloak,
  To protect him from farther harm.

Sleepy, and smiling, and free from care
  To her dainty crib, with pillows white,
Went the little maid with her dollies five,
  And the two Elizabeths kissed good-night.

JIM'S CIRCUS.

JIM was a drunkard, and Jane was his wife,
  With their children three, a wretched life
They lived in poverty, turmoil and strife,

In a poor little hut as you might pass,
With a broken gate and no flowers or grass,
And rags in the windows instead of glass.

The bed was straw and the coverlet torn,
The stove was rusty—a cover gone—
And chairs and table battered and worn.

The bread was brown, and the coffee was black,
Of meat there was always need and lack,
And meal and flour were scant in the sack.

Jane had hardly a decent gown,
And Jim's old hat had a hole in the crown,
While the children's shoes were the worst in town.

But Jim came home one night in glee,
" A circus is coming to town," said he,
" And, Jane, you must take the children three !"

63

"I've earned the money to-day," he cries,
While Jane looked up with mute surprise;
A smile on her lip, but tears in her eyes.

Then she bestirred herself with a will,
And mended their frocks with patient skill,
At her task the midnight found her still.

From her oldest gown she made aprons new,
And washed some faded ribbons blue,
For their braided locks of flaxen hue.

Then she combed her hair as she used when a girl,
With here and there a ringlet and curl,
And donned a brooch that she thought a pearl !

Then they all went forth and all were gay
As they joined the throng in the crowded way,
And Jim said, " Here with the children stay

"While I get the tickets.   I'll come back soon."
Then the band struck up a merry tune
And the hours wore on until it was noon.

Then, searching for him, her boy she sent,
Who fouud him at last, with money spent,
In drunken stupor beside the tent.

She gathered the children with burning smart
Of tortured love to her aching heart,
Transfixed with pity as with a dart.

God pity them all in their grief and woe,
Like a vision of beauty all aglow,
To their poor pinched lives seemed the paltry
show.

The tent was struck and its glories fled,
" *They hain't seen nothin' !* " she moaning said,
As home through the fields the way she led.

MOSES.

L EAVE for awhile your storybooks and play,
     And gather round me, children, while I tell
A tale which you may read in Holy Writ,
More wonderful and strange than aught you find
In thrilling legend or old-time romance.
My hero's name was Moses, and his home
In fertile Goshen where the river Nile
Through Egypt flows, whose tombs and pyramids
Her former power and glory still attest.
Born of a race oppressed and captive held,
His mother braved the tyrant's stern decree
That every male should at its birth be slain,
And for three months, by loving stratagem,
And every fond device her heart could prompt,
From jealous eyes did hide her beauteous babe.
But this could be no longer, and she took
Of reeds and rushes from the river's brink,
And deftly fashioned them with cunning hand
Into a cradle quaint and strange.   And then
She took the boy and robed him in the best
Her scanty store could furnish, twined his hair
In graceful ringlets, and with soft caress

Laid him therein and lulled him to his rest.
Amram was at his task, but Miriam
And Aaron knelt with her, and gave him there
Unto the keeping of their father's God.
Brave Miriam, the maiden, stayed behind
And watched to see what should become of him.
She hears the sound of merriment, and, lo!
With jest and laughter to the river's bank
Comes Egypt's youthful princess with her maids.
With eager eyes she scans the object strange
Nestled so safely 'mong the sheltering reeds,
And sends her maids to fetch it.   They obey,
And as she kneels beside it, the fair babe
Opens its eyes, and smiles, and stretches forth
Its dimpled hands to her, then at the sight
Of stranger's face, utters a wailing cry.
" This is a Hebrew child," the princess said;
"'So fair, he shall not die.   Too well I know
My royal father's edict, but to me,
His petted child, he is indulgent still,
Grants every wish and heeds my lightest whim."
She rose and looked around, and Miriam
Came with obeisance due, and stood demure
Before the princess, "Wilt thou that I go,"
With timid voice, she said, " and fetch for thee,
From the slave women one to nurse the child?
' Go!" was the answer, and the glad child ran
And brought her mother!   "Nurse this child and I,

Daughter of Egypt's king, will thee repay.
His name is Moses; surely I have drawn
Him from the water.   Give to him such care
As shall befit his station and his rank."
The child did grow in stature and in strength,
And was in Pharaoh's household as a son.
He learned all Egypt's wondrous lore; was skilled
In all its art and science; called the stars
Each by its name and marked its place in heaven;
Knew herbs and trees and called each flower by
        name;
Knew all the gods, their station and degree
And best of all knew Abraham's God, his own.
At length strange hopes and fears disquiet him,
Had God forgot his promise made of old?
He could not live in luxury and ease
And look each day upon his people's woe.
With his own hand he sought to avenge their
        wrong,
And, lo! they knew him not, but taunted him;
" Who made thee judge and ruler over us?"
Then Moses fled to the far wilderness,
And made his home with shepherds and their
        flocks,
Leading their quiet life for many years.
But God remembered him, and stayed his foot
In the lone desert.   A familiar bush
From twig and leaf gave forth strange, fiery points,

That grew, and twined, and wreathed themselves
    to flame,
Intense and bright and curling high and higher.
Awe-stricken, with dilated eyes he stood
To see the bush, burning yet unconsumed.
A voice called him by name, and talked with him,
And gave him high commission, to go forth
And in the name of Israel's God demand
Freedom for Israel to worship Him,
Of Egypt's haughty king. But Pharaoh said:
"Vex not the people with your idle tales,
I will not let them go, save to their tasks,
Are there no god's in Egypt? Wherefore then
Must they needs go to the far wilderness?"
So Pharaoh's heart was hardened. Then the Lord
Said unto Moses, "Take with thee thy rod
Thy brother Aaron, eloquent in speech,
Stand by the river's brink and stretch it forth."
And Moses did so. Straight the limpid wave
Curdled to blood, and blood was everywhere
Throughout the land, till Egypt loathed the sight.
Anon, at Moses' bidding, frogs came forth
In countless numbers till the land did groan.
Then, myraid flies did swarm in all the air,
And vermin crawled on beggar and on king.
Hot, burning boils distressed them. Pestilence
Did smite both man and beast. A grievous hail
Brake every herb and tree, and locusts came

In dark'ning clouds and each green thing devoured.
Then, o'er the ruined land a horror fell,
Darkness illumined by no ray of light.
Each in his place did sit and none could look
On the wan face of wife, or child, or friend.
And Pharaoh said to Moses, "'Tis enough,
Stay now thy hand, for Israel's God is Lord!
Go with thy people, sacrifice for me."
Yet again proud Pharaoh's heart was hardened.
Then the Lord spake unto Moses, "Take thy rod,
Lift it once more, and I will do a thing
Shall make the nations tremble. Go thou first
And sprinkle blood where'er my people dwell."
Then Moses took the rod of God, and stood
At midnight's hour and stretched it o'er the land,
The guilty land, and all its first born died!
The cherished prince, proud heir to Egypt's throne,
Lay dead within the palace! In the street
The beggar made his moan. A bitter cry
Rose from each household, and the king arose
And said to Moses, "Tarry not! Go forth!"
And the Egyptians hasted them; and gave
Them gold and jewels, whatsoe'er they asked.
'Twas a strange sight. Moses and Aaron stood
With all the Hebrew elders gathered there,
Each with his marshaled tribe, laden with spoil
That Egypt thrust upon them; beside
Women and children, with much store of goods,

And flocks and many cattle.   Far they stretched
Towards the wilderness.   Before them lay
The land of promise.   Behind them, Egypt,
With its years of toil and bitter bondage.
The bones of Joseph in their midst they bore,
An awful presence guided them; by day
Veiled in a cloud, majestic, dark and grand,
That changed and glowed and burned with fire by
    night.   -
Whither it led they followed, till at last
It rested by the sea.   And Pharaoh heard
And pondered much, and said, "Their God hath
    now
Deserted them, and they shall be our prey!
Up with the chariots !   bring these bondsmen back,
And Egypt's gods go with us to avenge !"
Dismay and terror filled the Hebrew camp.
"Why hast thou brought us here to perish thus ?"
Then Moses cried to God, and took the rod
From Aaron's hand and stretched it o'er the sea.
The mystic pillar stood between and shed
Light upon Israel's path, but on the foe
Darkness and gloom.   An east wind fiercely blew
Till the dry land appeared, and Israel passed
Dry shod where late the rolling waves had been.
Onward passed the Egyptian host, exultant
And secure.   An ominous hush was there,
And a great calm did fall upon the sea.

The waves slid to their place and overwhelmed
Chariots and horsemen in one common doom!
Thus Egpyt perished, but the Hebrews stood
With ranks unbroken on the farther shore,
While Miriam and Moses praised the Lord
Who wrought for them this great deliverance.

www.ingramcontent.com/pod-product-compliance
Lightning Source LLC
Chambersburg PA
CBHW032346020726
47499CB00009B/3181